92
Jul

Perez, Frank.

Raul Julia

DATE DUE	BORROWER'S NAME	ROOM NUMBER

92
Jul

Perez, Frank.

Raul Julia

Contemporary Hispanic Americans

RAUL JULIA

BY
FRANK PÉREZ AND ANN WEIL

RSVP

RAINTREE
STECK-VAUGHN
P U B L I S H E R S
The Steck-Vaughn Company

Austin, Texas

Published by Raintree Steck-Vaughn, an imprint of Steck-Vaughn Company.
Produced by Mega-Books, Inc.
Design and cover art by Michaelis/Carpelis Design Associates.
Cover photo: Retna Ltd.

Library of Congress Catologing-in-Publication Data
Pérez, Frank, 1956
    Raul Julia/by Frank Pérez and Ann Weil.
      p. cm. — (Contemporary Hispanic Americans)
    Includes bibliographical references and index.
    Summary: Narrates the life and career of the Puerto Rican born actor whose versatility was evident through thirty years of performances in the theater, movies, and television.
    ISBN 0-8172-3984-7
    ISBN 0-8114-9786-0 (softcover)
    1. Julia, Raul—Juvenile literature, 2. Actors—Puerto Rico—Biography—Juvenile literature.
3. Hispanic American actors—Biography—Juvenile literature. [1. Julia, Raul. 2. Actors and actresses. 3. Hispanic Americans—Biography.] I. Weil, Ann. II. Title. III. Series.
PN2434.J86P47 1995
792'.028'092—dc20   95-18549
[B]   CIP
                                             AC
Printed and bound in the United States.

1 2 3 4 5 6 7 8 9 LB 99 98 97 96 95

Photo Credits: Steve Granitz/Retna Ltd.: p. 4; I.P.A./Stills/Retna Ltd.: pp. 7, 39, 40; UPI/Bettmann: pp. 8, 17, 42; Ned Haines/Photo Researchers, Inc.: p.11; Martha Swope © TIME Inc.: p.13, 21, 22; Beryl Goldberg: p.14; Photofest: pp. 19, 33; D. Fineman/Sygma: p. 24; Robert Fuhring: p.26; Deweerot/Stills/Retna Ltd.: p. 29; Abolafia/Gamma Liaison: p.30; Gamma Liaison: pp. 35,44; Sygma: p.36.

Contents

Chapter One

IT'S SHOW TIME!

"It's show time!" Gomez Addams shouts in a scene from *The Addams Family* movie. For Raul Julia, the actor who played Gomez, it was also show time. It was his chance to show the world that he could play any **role**, whether comic or serious.

The Addams Family brought this Puerto Rican actor a new kind of stardom. However, Raul Julia was no "overnight success." For years, Raul Julia worked mainly in theater in New York City. He did everything from street theater, where actors perform plays on neighborhood sidewalks, to smash hits on Broadway.

Then Raul branched out into films. During his thirty-year career, he acted in more than thirty movies. Raul starred in low-cost films made for Spanish-speaking audiences and performed in multimillion-

Raul Julia's talent and spirit won him the love of hundreds of friends and millions of fans.

dollar Hollywood **productions**. He played good guys and bad guys and just plain guys. The two *Addams Family* movies won Raul many new fans, especially among young people. However, many others had already known that Raul Julia was a great actor.

Raul was not only a great actor, but also a very versatile one. A versatile actor is one who can play many different kinds of characters and make people believe they are real. Raul was also a good singer. His deep voice could express many feelings. He was tall—over six feet—and very handsome, too. His most distinctive feature were his large, hooded, gray eyes.

In spite of his good looks and many talents, Raul faced a number of challenges on his road to stardom. When he started out, Raul was usually **cast** as a Hispanic character in both English and Spanish-language plays. A young, struggling actor cannot be picky about his roles. Most are pleased to get any work at all. Yet Raul knew early on that he had to fight against being typecast. Typecasting is when an actor keeps playing the same "type" of role, usually because of his or her looks, speech, or background.

Raul wanted to be free to play many different types of roles. He did not believe his career should be limited because he was Puerto Rican. "I came [to New York] to be an actor," he said. "I didn't come here to be a stereotype." Raul believed that an actor should have "the opportunity to prove that he can play any role, whether it's part of his background or not."

Raul Julia's comic genius in *The Addams Family and Addams Family Values* brought him to a new level of stardom.

Some actors with the same goals might have tried to "pass" as non-Hispanic, but not Raul. He was always extremely proud of his Puerto Rican heritage. A close friend joked that Raul wore the map of Puerto Rico on his forehead. She said, "He wanted everyone to know he was Puerto Rican." Many actors change their names, especially when the names are difficult to pronounce or sound "ethnic." For example, another Hispanic actor, Martin Sheen, changed his last name from Estevez. His son, actor Emilio Estevez, went back to his father's original last name. Raul Julia's name identified him as Hispanic, but he never even considered changing it.

Theater was Raul Julia's first love, and he never gave up acting on stage. Here, he stars in the hit Broadway musical *Nine*.

Raul took voice classes to improve his speech. He also learned how to speak with a British accent, or with no accent at all. Yet Raul never tried to hide his own accent, even when he could. This decision not to lose his distinctive Puerto Rican accent made it more difficult for him to get roles. People assumed that because Raul's voice sounded Hispanic, he could not play non-Hispanic characters.

Raul Julia successfully fought against being stereotyped as a Puerto Rican actor. He did this without abandoning his heritage, changing his name, or giving up his accent. He refused to become someone else's idea of what an actor should be. Raul achieved stardom on his own terms.

Many actors who start out in the theater move to Hollywood when they become successful. They never work in the theater again. Instead, they appear only in films where they have starring roles. They demand huge salaries and buy lavish homes and fancy cars. Raul, however, selected the roles he liked, not only the ones that paid a lot. His first true love was the theater, and as a result, he stayed in New York. He lived in an apartment on the Upper West Side of Manhattan. He also bought a farm in the Catskill Mountains, a few hours from the city. There, he and his family could get away and enjoy the country.

People in his Manhattan neighborhood knew him as a friendly, open man, a family man who was devoted to his wife and their two sons. He didn't surround himself with bodyguards to shield him from the public. After all, the people were his audience. He wasn't in show business for the money or the awards. He was in it for the thrill of acting in front of an audience. He loved to make believe, to pretend. And it all began when he was still a young boy living in Puerto Rico.

Chapter Two

GROWING UP IN PUERTO RICO

Raul Rafael Carlos Julia y Arcelay was born on March 9, 1940, in San Juan, Puerto Rico. Puerto Rico is a small island in the Caribbean Sea. The island has many beautiful sandy beaches. The weather is warm year-round, which makes it a popular vacation spot for tourists from all over the world.

Raul's family was well off, and Raul grew up in the suburbs of San Juan, Puerto Rico's capital. His mother, Olga Arcelay, was an amateur singer. His father, whose name is also Raul Julia, owned a successful restaurant.

The family traveled often to Europe, and Raul attended the best schools in Puerto Rico. Raul's family was Roman Catholic, and young Raul attended a grade school run by North American nuns. His teachers spoke little Spanish, so Raul learned English at school. At home, he and his family spoke Spanish.

Young Raul made his acting **debut** in the first grade. He played the part of the devil in a class play.

Raul Julia was born and raised close to San Juan. Many of the buildings in the Puerto Rican capital, including its city hall, are hundreds of years old.

Instead of just walking out on the stage and saying his lines, Raul decided to try something different. He shrieked as loud as he could, threw himself on the floor, and rolled around.

He hadn't rehearsed this way, and his family and the teachers were stunned. They thought he was having some sort of fit. But Raul was acting. After he shocked the audience with this grand entrance, he stood up and said his lines. "It was a marvelous experience in which I entered and let go of myself," he later remembered. "I became sort of like possessed or something."

As a boy, Raul loved to make-believe. He was also a bit of a prankster who liked to fool people. There was a piano next to a window in his family's house. Raul knew that people could look in and see him when he played. So he put on a record of classical piano music and turned up the volume very loud. Then he sat at the piano and pretended to play music. People would stop and stare at him through the window. They were amazed that a young child could play so beautifully! Even then, Raul Julia loved to have an audience.

Raul attended San Ignacio de Loyola High School in San Juan. There he was first exposed to the plays of William Shakespeare, one of the greatest writers of all time. Shakespeare, who lived in England about 400 years ago, wrote in verse, like poetry. His plays can be difficult to understand at first. Students at San Ignacio read Shakespeare aloud in class and performed his plays. Raul learned the rhythms and meaning of Shakespeare's words. He found them beautiful and powerful. This experience in high school had an important effect on the rest of his life.

After high school, Raul enrolled at the University of Puerto Rico. His parents wanted him to study law, but he preferred acting. Raul had known ever since he was five that he wanted to act. He had been in every school play throughout grade school and high school, and didn't want to give that up. Raul looked inside of himself and asked, "Are you going to do what you enjoy, which is theater, or are you going to go to law

In high school, Raul Julia learned to love the plays of William Shakespeare. One day, he would perform in many of these same plays, including *The Tempest.*

school?" He decided to do what he loved, and his parents supported his decision.

Raul continued acting in college plays. During his college years, he also spent some time studying at Fordham College in New York City. It was while he was in New York that he received some tragic news. His younger brother had been killed in a car crash. His brother's tragic death had a great effect on Raul. It was a loss he never forgot. "You do your best not to carry it around as a burden," Raul later said. "But you

Raul Julia attended the University of Puerto Rico in San Juan, where he acted in many college plays.

feel a lot of guilt. You wonder, 'Why him and not me?'"

After graduating from the University of Puerto Rico, Raul Julia became involved with the theater scene in San Juan. His love of Shakespeare led him to appear in an amateur, or nonprofessional, production of Shakespeare's tragedy *Macbeth*. This play is about a nobleman in Scotland, and a lot of the action takes place in a castle. It was performed in an ancient fortress in the old section of San Juan. In addition to plays, Raul appeared in nightclub acts, called **revues**.

Raul was doing a revue at a San Juan Hotel when he was "discovered" by the actor and comedian Orson

Bean. Orson describes the first time he saw Raul Julia: "I saw Raul in a revue he and a few others were putting on in a hotel where I was staying. He stood out so much, and I spoke to him afterwards. I told him I thought he was incredibly talented. He said he was planning to go to Europe to pursue acting. I suggested that he try New York instead."

Raul Julia took Orson Bean's advice. In 1964, when he was 24 years old, he moved to New York City to become a professional actor.

Chapter Three

BEGINNING IN THE THEATER

Orson Bean had given Raul Julia his phone number in New York. When Raul arrived in the city, Orson helped the young actor find an apartment. He also introduced Raul to Wyn Handman, who had been Orson's acting teacher.

Raul immediately signed up for lessons with Wyn Handman. Wyn noticed Raul's talent right away. He said: "Even back then, he had incredible charm when he acted. He was also very serious about it, and even when he had a thick accent, he would be doing speeches from *Othello* in order to perfect himself." *Othello* is one of Shakespeare's most famous plays.

New York City's largest and most famous theaters are located in a district near Broadway, a long avenue that runs through the city. There are also thousands of smaller theaters in New York. These are called Off-Broadway. They provide the most opportunities for young actors just starting out. Raul had an advantage over most of the other young actors because he could speak both English and Spanish. New York City has many Hispanic people who speak Spanish, and there are quite a few productions especially for them.

Raul shared a one-room apartment on the Upper West Side of Manhattan with another actor. Raul's parents sent him money for food and rent so that he could devote himself to finding work as an actor. It did not take him long. On March 17, 1964, he made his New York debut. He played Astolfo, the king's nephew, in a Spanish-language production of *Life Is a Dream,* by the great Spanish writer Pedro Calderón de la Barca.

Now Raul was able to join Actors Equity, a union

Raul Julia got his start in Spanish-language productions. His first New York role was in *Life is a Dream.*

for professional actors. Raul's career was on its way. Proudly, he told his parents that he would now support himself. Actually, he was not making much money as an actor, even when he was working. What's more, an actor never knows when he will get his next job—and his next paycheck. Despite these hardships, Raul was thrilled to be living his dream. He was a professional actor!

Raul joined a company called Theater in the Street, which staged plays in English and Spanish in poor neighborhoods. Plays were performed from a truck that converted into a stage. Theater in the Street was bringing theater to people who could not afford to go see a Broadway show. These were tough audiences who weren't shy about expressing themselves. When they liked the play, they would laugh loudly and yell their approval. But sometimes, when they didn't like or understand what was going on, they would throw things at the actors.

Carla Pinza acted with Raul in several productions. She is Puerto Rican, too, but was born and raised in New York City. She describes working with Raul in Theater in the Street: "Raul wasn't street-smart the way American-born Puerto Ricans often are. He was naive and had that wonderful quality that people from the island bring with them."

At first, Raul was scared by the rough neighborhoods. Before long, however, he developed a good relationship with his audience, especially its younger

Raul Julia and Carla Pinza would act together in many productions, including Shakespeare's *Two Gentlemen of Verona*.

members. "The children loved him," Carla said. "They would follow him offstage when he made his exit and ask him about the play. Raul would explain what was going on and tell them to go back and watch the play and pay attention to what was happening on stage."

While Raul was working with Theater in the Street,

Orson Bean introduced him to a friend. This young woman was struck by Raul's good looks and sweet nature. She recalls meeting him at a restaurant soon after he arrived in New York: "He was extremely handsome. He was quite shy, even timid, especially around women. He was doing street theater at the time, and his English wasn't so great, but he was charming and sweet. I noticed at least one woman was very interested in him that evening, but Raul was engaged to someone back in Puerto Rico." Raul and his Puerto Rican fiancée did get married. She was his childhood sweetheart and the daughter of friends of his family. Unfortunately, the marriage didn't work out, and they were divorced after four years.

Raul continued to get roles mostly in Spanish-language productions. He worked with the Puerto Rican Traveling Theater. He still spoke English with a thick Puerto Rican accent, and he often mixed in Spanish words with English. An actor must be able to control his voice, and as Raul continued to study, his English improved.

In December 1966, Raul got a good review for his work in a play called *The Ox Cart*. The play is about a Puerto Rican family and how they adapt to life in the mainland United States. Raul was cast as a young member of the family. It was a role not so different from Raul's own experience!

In 1966, Raul met Joseph Papp, a man who would play an important part in Raul's acting career. Joe Papp

Producer Joseph Papp brought free theater to thousands of New Yorkers. He also recognized the talent of young Raul Julia.

was a special kind of **producer**. He was committed to bringing plays to everyone. He believed people should have the opportunity to see a live performance, even if they did not have much money. Like Theater in the Street, Joe Papp had a mobile-unit that brought theater directly to the people. He also founded the New York Shakespeare Festival (NYSF), an organization that is still going strong today. NYSF puts on plays every summer at the Delacorte Theater, an outdoor theater in New York's Central Park. Tickets are free.

In the summer of 1966, Joe Papp was doing a Spanish-language production of Shakespeare's *Macbeth* with the mobile unit. Raul got a part in the play. "We traveled all over the neighborhoods with this truck that turned into a stage," he said. For Raul, it was a special experience. "We were bringing theater to people that had never gone to the theater before," he said.

Later, Raul read at a Puerto Rican poetry festival at the Delacorte Theater. Raul recalled: "It was a very patriotic poem, and I got really inspired and the audience went wild." Joe Papp was there, and he

Raul Julia would eventually star in many Shakespeare plays for the NYSF, including *Othello* in 1979. For this role, Raul used makeup to darken his face. Othello was a Moor from North Africa and a victorious general in the army of Venice.

remembered the gifted young actor. Raul auditioned again for Joe and was given a small part in another Shakespeare play. "That was my dream come true," Raul said.

Even with these early successes, Raul did not always have acting work. Most actors sometimes have to get other part-time work to make money. Raul was no exception. He taught Spanish. He also tried selling magazine subscriptions. He even took a course to sell pens in grocery stores. None of these jobs worked out. He was desperate for work and decided to call Joe Papp and ask him for a full-time job.

Joe Papp produced so many shows each year that he could not get to know all the actors personally. Raul was not sure whether Joe Papp would remember him. "I paced up and down in my apartment for a long time, to gather up the strength to call." Raul told Joe Papp that he would do any job, "as long as it's in the theater." Joe Papp offered him a job as a house manager. As house manager, Raul made sure everything went smoothly at the performances.

Soon Raul Julia became a regular actor in NYSF productions. "I practically lived there," he said. He performed in the plays the NYSF staged each summer. Playing Shakespeare helped Raul avoid being typecast as a Hispanic actor who could only be in Spanish-language plays. He had the opportunity to create characters very different from himself.

Raul made his Broadway debut a year later, in

By the end of the 1960s, Raul Julia's career was beginning to take off. His talent and hard work would soon lead to many roles in theater, film, and television.

September 1968. He played a servant in a play called *The Cuban Thing*, about Fidel Castro's revolution in Cuba. Unfortunately, the play closed after a few weeks. Raul's acting, however, caught people's attention. He began to get offers of more important roles. He played a Latin American revolutionary running from the law in an Off-Broadway comedy called *The Castro Complex*. Although the play was not well-reviewed, Raul was. One **critic** wrote: "He has a future—in better plays." Raul did have a great future ahead of him in the theater—and in movies and television, as well.

Chapter

ON BROADWAY

Raul had small parts in three movies that came out in 1971. He also worked on the television soap opera "Love of Life." His favorite job in the early seventies, however, was working on "Sesame Street."

At that time, the award-winning educational show had been on the air for about a year. "Sesame Street" wanted to expand its Hispanic characters. People felt the show should include skits that were bilingual, in both English and Spanish. Raul auditioned for Cis Corman, who was in charge of casting. She was impressed with his audition and gave him the role of Rafael. Cis Corman said: "He had a presence, and he really wanted to do 'Sesame Street.' He wanted to work on a children's show. He cared about kids, especially minority kids."

Raul's character, Rafael, ran a fix-it shop with another character named Luis. Emilio Delgado, who played Luis, said: "Latinos were just beginning to come

Raul Julia loved working with children and enjoyed his role on "Sesame Street" in the early 1970s.

on. Finally we were recognized and could get work and do good things. Raul was very much a part of that. He was a pioneer for all of us."

Sonia Manzano played Maria on "Sesame Street" when Raul was on the show. Sonia remembers how Raul worked with the kids on the show, many of whom were not professional actors: "Raul was always making them giggle. Once, he was supposed to make the letter *L* with a fold-out carpenter's ruler, but he wasn't holding it straight, and it looked more like a *V*. The kids thought that was hysterical. They teased him about it as the scene was going on. But Raul just laughed and corrected himself on camera."

At the same time he was working on "Sesame Street," Raul was also performing on Broadway. He had the leading role in the NYSF's *Two Gentlemen of Verona*. This comic play by Shakespeare had been at the Delacorte Theater in Central Park that summer, but it was so popular that Joe Papp later moved the production to a Broadway theater.

Emilio Delgado, who worked with Raul on "Sesame Street," also happened to be Raul's understudy for the role of Proteus in *Two Gentlemen of Verona*. An understudy takes over the role if the actor is sick and can't perform. But Emilio never went on for Raul. "Raul was one of the healthiest men in show business," Emilio says. Raul was also one of the hardest working men in show business. He was kept very busy acting on "Sesame Street" during the day and on Broadway in the evenings. Emilio recalls: "Sometimes, he'd fall asleep in the make-up chair. But he always put his all into everything he did. He gave 100 percent whether it was a song or a bit with me or the kids."

Two Gentlemen of Verona was a great success. It was also a big turning point for Raul. He received his first Tony Award nomination, for best actor in a musical. The Tonys are given out each year to the best people in theater. Raul did not win the award, but he felt happy just being nominated.

Raul was still performing in *Two Gentlemen of Verona* on Broadway the next summer. At the same time, he began acting in Shakespeare's *Hamlet* in Central Park. Raul played Osric, who doesn't appear until the last act. So, for several hectic weeks, Raul was whisked by limousine from Broadway to Central Park in time for his appearance. Despite this rushing around, Raul received very good reviews for his performance in *Hamlet.*

Not everything Raul did was a hit, though. He starred in a space-age musical called *Via Galactica,* which closed after one week. Raul quickly rebounded. In the summer of 1973, he acted in two Shakespeare plays at the Delacorte Theater: *As You Like It* and *King Lear.* Once again, he had come home to Shakespeare.

In an interview, Raul described his deep love and respect for Shakespeare's work: "I love the rhythm, the music, the poetry. I make it my own. I become a poet and I just see Shakespeare smiling at me."

Not all the critics were smiling at Raul for his performance as Orlando in *As You Like It,* which is a comedy. A few critics didn't like Raul's interpretation of his role, complete with a Spanish accent. Others admired the way he spoke Shakespeare's lines, as one critic wrote, "with an individual magic of voice and eyes." In the tragedy *King Lear,* Raul played the evil Edmund. The play was so successful that it was broadcast on public television.

Raul started performing in more starring roles in Broadway theaters. In 1974 he received his second Tony nomination. He played a college student who impersonates his aunt in the musical *Where's Charley?* He was nominated for a third Tony for the NYSF production of *The Threepenny Opera* by Bertolt

Raul enjoyed playing villains as well as heroes. Here, he stars as the evil Mack the Knife in *The Threepenny Opera*.

Brecht. In this play, Raul played a criminal called Mack the Knife. Many critics considered this to be Raul's best performance in years. Raul enjoyed the challenge of playing an evil villain. "I remember learning that even evil thoughts were a sin," he said. As an actor, however, Raul could express evil feelings through art.

Raul's next role was in *The Cherry Orchard*. This is a serious play by Anton Chekhov, a Russian writer. On opening night, a group of teenagers laughed wildly throughout the play. Some of the audience found them annoying, but onstage, Raul did not. He didn't

Raul Julia married dancer Merel Poloway in 1976. Here, the couple attends the 1991 Tony Awards ceremony.

mind that the teenagers found the play very funny. He respected whatever they felt about the performance. Besides, Raul was used to audience participation from his days with Theater in the Street. At least this time no one threw anything at him!

Although most of his theater work was in New York City, Raul also performed plays "on the road." Sometimes a theater company will travel from city to city so people all over the country can see a popular play. This is called a touring company. In mid-1978, Raul put on a huge black cape to portray the vampire in a touring company production of *Dracula*. His *Dracula* was so popular with audiences that a year later Raul was chosen to play the role on Broadway.

Raul continued to spend his summers at the Delacorte Theater with the NYSF. In 1979 he starred in *Othello*, a personal favorite since his early days in acting class. Raul played Othello, a jealous husband who kills his wife and then regrets what he has done. His powerful performance received rave reviews.

In January 1980, Raul returned to Broadway to play a cool and proper Englishman in *Betrayal*. To prepare for this role, Raul spent several weeks in London. He hired a voice coach to help him master the upper-class British accent. He then starred in the Broadway musical hit *Nine*. This performance won Raul his fourth Tony Award nomination.

Raul's personal life was also going very well. In 1976 he had married Merel Poloway, a dancer whom he had met while they were working together in a musical. The couple eventually would have two sons: Raul and Benjamin. Raul was now a successful stage actor and a very happily married man. His career was on a roll. The next stop would be Hollywood!

Chapter Five

HOLLYWOOD

Raul Julia had become a great success on the New York stage. Yet it took a long time for him to be taken seriously in Hollywood. In the late 1970s, he still had not had a major movie role. Raul was interested in doing movies, but only if the parts were as good as the ones he got in the theater. He felt that in Hollywood, he might be more limited because he was Puerto Rican. "I'd rather not work than be typecast and do the same things over and over," he said.

Raul had his first starring role on screen in the 1985 movie *Kiss of the Spider Woman*. He played Valentin, a political prisoner in South America. Political prisoners are people who are in jail because of their political beliefs. There, they are sometimes starved or beaten. To prepare for this role, Raul talked to people who had been tortured by the army in Brazil. He said: "I needed to know what the feelings and emotions were of a person who had gone through that."

Raul Julia with William Hurt in a scene from the 1985 movie *Kiss of the Spider Woman*. Both men won high praise for their powerful performances.

In *Kiss of the Spider Woman*, Valentin must share a cell with a man who is gay. The gay prisoner was played in the movie by William Hurt. The two prisoners are very different, but they learn to respect each other. Raul liked the film's story immediately. It reflected many of his own beliefs. He said: "It's something beyond just entertainment. *Kiss of the Spider Woman* gets people to think and perhaps deal with their own prejudices."

To play his part, Raul had to lose some weight. Raul ended up losing over thirty pounds to look like the starving Valentin. How did he manage to do it? First, he explained, he stopped eating fattening foods. Then, he slowly reduced his intake of all foods. "By the time we began shooting, I was eating very small quantities of food," he said. He stayed on this diet for four months. "There was no problem gaining it back," said Raul.

During the 1980s, Raul Julia was a very busy actor. Not all his work was in big Hollywood pictures. Raul appeared in two movies produced by Zaga Films, a Puerto Rican production company. He knew these films would not further his career or make him a lot of money. He just wanted to show his support for this small film company from his native island.

His final movie of the 1980s was the most meaningful for Raul. In *Romero*, he played Archbishop Oscar Romero of El Salvador, who was assassinated in 1980. At the time of Romero's murder, El Salvador was in the middle of a civil war. During the war, the Salvadoran government was responsible for torturing and murdering people. Romero spoke out against these cruel practices and was killed for it. To prepare for the movie, Raul listened to tapes of sermons and diaries kept by Archbishop Romero. He said, "I had a responsibility to do justice to this man, this hero, this giant, this saint."

Not many people saw the movie. Perhaps the story of a real-life murdered priest sounded too depressing. *Romero* was not a box-office smash, which was disappointing for Raul. He thought this movie could help educate people. When *Romero* was released on

Raul Julia had strong feelings about his role in the film *Romero*, about a Salvadoran priest who stood up to the government of his country.

videocassette, Raul said, "I hope this picture will help wake people up to what's happening in Central America." He expressed his wish that people would get together to watch and discuss the video.

Not all of Raul's film efforts were so serious. He played many different types of roles and found something worthwhile in them all. He said that he would consider any part, "as long as it is something that has some beauty, some quality. I think everything I've done has had that."

Raul played lawyer Sandy Stern in the hit movie *Presumed Innocent*. It was fun for him to pretend to

be a lawyer, the career his parents had hoped he would choose for himself. While working on this role, he found out that lawyers and actors have a lot in common. Both are performers. Actors perform on stage and in front of movie cameras. Lawyers perform in court, where their audience is the judge and jury.

By the end of the 1980s, Raul had worked up to starring roles in movies—just in time to play Gomez Addams. Barry Sonnenfeld, the **director** of the film, thought Raul was a natural choice for the part. "Raul was born to play Gomez. He loves his wife, he loves his children, he loves life. He loves acting."

Barry Sonnenfeld wasn't the only one who liked Raul for the role of Gomez. Anjelica Huston, who played Gomez's wife, Morticia, was also pleased. Anjelica asked Barry Sonnenfeld who he was thinking of for the part of Gomez. "When I said 'Raul Julia,' her eyes lit up, and she said, 'Perfect,'" Sonnenfeld recalled. Raul and Anjelica were both perfect. *The Addams Family* was such a hit that they made a sequel, *Addams Family Values*, released in 1993. The *Addams Family* movies cemented Raul Julia's position in Hollywood. He was definitely a movie star. Sadly, this star would fall from the sky too soon.

As Gomez and Morticia Addams, Raul Julia and Anjelica Huston won the hearts of thousands of fans nationwide.

Chapter Six

THE CURTAIN FALLS

In the fall of 1994, Raul Julia had a massive stroke that left him in a coma. Friends and fans across the country gave him their hopes and prayers, but tragically, he never recovered. He died after only a few days on October 24, 1994, at the age of 54.

There were memorial services for Raul Julia in New York City and Los Angeles. He had a state funeral in Puerto Rico. At this service, Ruben Berrios, a member of the Puerto Rican Senate, expressed what many in the Hispanic-American community felt. He said that Raul was the "luminous mirror in which Puerto Ricans see the best of themselves." Puerto Rico was as proud of Raul as he had been of his heritage.

Raul had a long and productive career. On film he portrayed a wide variety of characters very different from himself. He played an Italian race-car driver in *The Gumball Rally* (1976). He was a crazed villain in *The Escape Artist* (1982) and a romantic waiter in

One From the Heart (1982). He starred as a police detective in *Compromising Positions* (1985).

Raul also enjoyed playing Hispanic characters as long as they were not stereotypes. In *The Morning After* (1986), Raul played a Los Angeles hairdresser who fights to overcome prejudice. In *The Penitent* (1988), Raul played Ramon, a young peasant in New Mexico. In the comedy *Moon over Parador* (1988), which takes place on an imaginary Caribbean island, Raul dyed his hair blond to play the Hispanic-German head of the police force. In *Tequila Sunrise* (1988), Raul played a Hispanic drug dealer who loves opera. In *Havana* (1990), he played a Cuban rebel leader.

Raul had not been looking well for a while before his

In his career, Raul Julia showed the world that he could play any kind of role. Here, he stars in the 1990 film *Havana.*

stroke. His family kept his medical condition private. Still, some friends sensed that Raul knew he didn't have much time left. Raul seemed to choose projects that were especially meaningful to him during his last few years.

Raul's final television role was in *The Burning Season*. It was broadcast on HBO a month before his death. Raul played a man named Chico Mendes, who was fighting to save the Amazon rain forest. Mendes was murdered by people who opposed his cause. Like the story of Romero, this was something Raul felt was important for people to know. Raul had already died when he won a Golden Globe award for his portrayal of Mendes. His wife, Merel Poloway, accepted this very special award on his behalf.

Raul's last motion picture was *Street Fighter*, which was released after his death. *Street Fighter* is based on a popular video game. Raul's two young sons, Raul and Benjamin, loved the game and were thrilled that their dad was going to play the villain, Bison. They told him all about the character and even helped him prepare for his role. Even the filming was a family event. The boys and their mother joined Raul on the set.

Raul was very much a family man. Although he was very busy working on movies and in the theater, he made sure he spent a lot of time with his sons. One year he took his older son to Boy Scout camp. Everyone knew he was a celebrity and wanted him to perform for them. But Raul wanted to be just another dad at camp. He was there to do things with his son, not to be a star. In the evenings, he sang and told stories around the campfire. His son had a great time at camp and felt really proud of his dad. Raul had managed to keep the experience a very personal one for him and for his son.

Raul especially enjoyed spending the holidays with his family. These occasions were more important to him than any acting job. His religion and spirituality were also very meaningful for him. He was raised in a Catholic home, and that religion was important to him when he was young. But Raul had an open mind and learned about other faiths and beliefs as well.

His desire to learn more about himself drove Raul to attend a self-improvement program called Erhard Seminars Training, known as est. Raul felt that est helped him to understand himself better and to overcome obstacles in his career and personal life. Raul became friends with Werner Erhard, who created est.

In 1977, Erhard created the Hunger Project. Its goal is to end world hunger by the year 2000. Raul became one of the Hunger Project's biggest supporters. Raul

Raul Julia devoted much of his time to helping others. He was especially dedicated to the Hunger Project.

believed that human beings had the means to end hunger, as long as they made it a priority. After his family and his work, Raul did make the Hunger Project his personal priority. He even fasted one day a month as a statement about world hunger.

This dedicated man also gave a lot of his time to promoting Hispanic culture by helping Hispanic-Americans in the arts. Raul was active with the Hispanic Organization of Latin Actors (HOLA). He also co-founded The Latino Playwrights Reading Workshop with Carla Pinza to help Hispanic-American film and television writers develop their work. He appeared at fund-raisers for Hispanic theater companies. He even promoted tourism for his native Puerto Rico.

Raul had a special place in his heart for young people. He was especially concerned about the rising rate of teen violence. To do something about that, he co-sponsored a scriptwriting competition for high school students. He knew teenagers had a lot of anger inside them. Raul encouraged teenagers to express their emotions through art rather than through violence. He told a gathering of high school students: "If you want to express your anger, write it down. If you want to murder your father or throw your mother out the window, write it down—because then it becomes art instead of tragedy." A New York City newspaper reported this story under the headline: "Teens told to shoot films, not people."

Although Raul won the respect of his fellow actors

Raul Julia loved his last Broadway role, as Don Quixote in *Man of La Mancha*. He said of the part, "We are all dreamers."

and the love of his fans, he did not win many awards. He was nominated four times for Tony Awards for his work on Broadway, but he never won. After failing to win for the fourth time, Raul remarked that in the United States, a great deal of importance is placed on winning. "But there's something beyond winning or losing," he said, "which is just celebrating."

That was truly his attitude. Raul Julia celebrated life! Part of him was still the little boy pretending to play the piano for his astonished neighbors. He once said, "Acting is about giving. The greater the acting, the greater the giving." He was certainly a generous man in his own life as well as in his work.

Raul's last role on the New York stage was not Shakespeare. In some ways, however, it was even more meaningful for him. In 1992 he played Don Quixote in the musical *Man of La Mancha*. The musical is based on the novel *Don Quixote* by the great Spanish writer Miguel de Cervantes. Raul was very pleased that he had been offered the role of Don Quixote. It had previously been played by one of Raul's idols, actor José Ferrer, who was also from Puerto Rico.

In the musical, Don Quixote, a country gentleman, thinks he is a knight. He goes off to travel through the countryside and defend people's honor. Many of the people he meets think he is a silly fool. But Don Quixote dreams that the world could be a better place. Raul said, "We all have Don Quixote inside of us. We are all dreamers. We would all like to see a better world. We all would like to make a difference." Raul Julia certainly did make a difference.

1940 Born in Puerto Rico on March 9.

1964 Moves to New York City to become an actor. Makes New York debut in a Spanish-language production of *Life is a Dream*.

1968 Makes Broadway debut in *The Cuban Thing*.

1971 Gets first movie and TV roles, including "Sesame Street." Receives the first of four Tony award nominations for the hit *Two Gentlemen of Verona*.

1976 Marries Merel Poloway.

1978 Plays the lead in *Dracula* on Broadway.

1979 Stars in the New York Shakespeare Festival's production of *Othello*.

1985 Has first starring movie role, in *Kiss of the Spider Woman*.

1991 Plays Gomez Addams in the movie *The Addams Family*.

1992 Stars in *Man of La Mancha* on Broadway.

1993 Stars in *Addams Family Values*.

1994 Dies on October 24, in New York City.

Glossary

cast The role an actor is given, or the group of actors who appear in a play or movie.

critic Someone who reviews performances.

debut An actor's first appearance.

director The person who supervises the acting, lighting, music, and rehearsals for a play or movie.

producer The person who supervises or finances the making of a movie, TV show, or play.

production A performance, such as a play, movie, or TV show.

revue An act consisting of skits, dancing, and music, often performed in clubs.

role The character or part an actor plays.

Bibliography

Hadley-Garcia, George. *Hispanic Hollywood.* New York: Carol, 1990.

Hoban, Phobe. "Meeting Raul." *New York,* November 25, 1991.

Larsen, Ronald J. *The Puerto Ricans in America.* New York: Lerner, 1989.

Stetoff, Rebecca. *Raul Julia.* New York: Chelsea House, 1994.

Index